The Ladybird Key Words Reading Scheme is based on these commonly used words. Those used most often in the English language are introduced first—with other words of popular appeal to children. All the Key Words list is covered in the early books, and the later titles use further word lists to develop full reading fluency. The total number of different words which will be learned in the complete reading scheme is nearly two thousand. The gradual introduction of these words, frequent repetition and complete 'carry-over' from book to book, will ensure rapid learning.

The full colour illustrations have been designed to create a desirable attitude towards learning— by making every child *eager* to read each title. Thus this attractive reading scheme embraces not only the latest findings in word frequency, but also the natural interests and activities of happy children.

Each book contains a list of the new words introduced.

*W MURRAY, the author of the Ladybird Key Words Reading Scheme, is an experienced headmaster, author and lecturer on the teaching of reading. He is co-author, with J McNally, of* Key Words to Literacy — *a teacher's book published by The Teacher Publishing Co Ltd.*

**THE LADYBIRD KEY WORDS READING SCHEME** has 12 graded books in each of its three series — 'a', 'b' and 'c'. As explained in the handbook *Teaching Reading*, these 36 graded books are all written on a controlled vocabulary, and take the learner from the earliest stages of reading to reading fluency.

The 'a' series gradually introduces and repeats new words. The parallel 'b' series gives the needed further repetition of these words at each stage, but in a different context and with different illustrations.

The 'c' series is also parallel to the 'a' series, and supplies the necessary link with writing and phonic training.

An illustrated booklet — *Notes for using the Ladybird Key Words Reading Scheme* — can be obtained free from the publishers. This booklet fully explains the Key Words principle. It also includes information on the reading books, work books and apparatus available, and such details as the vocabulary loading and reading ages of all books.

**BOOK 2b**

The Ladybird Key Words Reading Scheme

# Have a go

*by* W MURRAY

*with illustrations*
*by* MARTIN AITCHISON

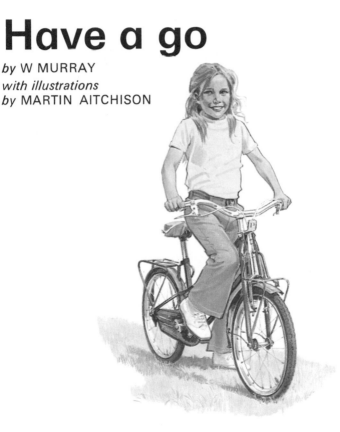

Ladybird Books Loughborough

I like the dog.

You like the dog.

You and I like the dog.

you    You

I like trees.

You like trees.

You and I like trees.

You want toys.

I want toys.

You and I want toys.

want

You like Peter.

I like Peter.

We like Peter.

we  We

I like Jane.

You like Jane.

We like Jane.

Jane

Here are shops.

We like shops.

We like toy shops.

are

You can fish.

I can fish.

We can fish.

---

can   fish

You want fun.

I want fun.

This is fun.

**fun   this   This**

This is Pat.

I like Pat.

Pat likes fun.

We like this dog.

**Pat**

# Here is some water.

some    water

I like the water.
Here is Peter
and here is Jane.

Here you are,
Jane and Peter.

Here is some water.

Look in the water.

You are in the water.

---

look  Look

Here is Peter.

He likes water.

He has the dog.

The dog is
in the water.

He likes it.

he  **He**  it

# Jane has a ball.

It is for Pat.

Pat is here.

He wants the ball.

for

Here is a tree.

Pat looks into the tree.

He looks for Peter
and Jane.

They are in the tree.

into    they    They

Look here, says Jane.

Look here, Peter.

Come and look.

Peter comes, and
they look.

Here are some sweets.

Some are for Peter
and some for Jane.

They have some sweets

They like sweets.

sweets    have

Peter wants to jump
and Pat wants to jump.

They jump for fun.

Can you jump this?
says Peter to Jane.

to    jump

Yes, says Jane.
Yes, I can jump this.

I want to jump.

Look, Peter, look.

I can jump this.

yes   Yes

Peter and Jane
go to the shop.
They go into the shop
for some fish.

Peter has the dog,
and Jane has the fish.

The fish go into the water.

Into the water they go.

Pat wants the fish.

no No

No, Pat, no, says Peter.

No, no, no, says Jane
to the dog.

Peter and Jane have fun

Here comes Peter .

Here comes Jane .

Here they come .

We like this, they say .

Have a go,
says Jane to Peter.

Yes, says Peter.

He has a go.
You have a go,
says Peter to Jane.
Jane has a go.

Have some,
says Jane to Peter.

Yes, says Peter.

You have some, Jane
says Peter.

Yes, I like it, Jane says.

ICES

49

Here they go.

Jane wants to go home
Peter wants to go home
and the dog wants
to go home.

Yes, we want to go home,
they say.

**home**

## Words used in this book

Total number of new words 27

Now use book 2c